This Book Belongs To:

_____

First published in the United States, Great Britain, Canada, Australia, and
New Zealand in 2014 by NorthSouth Books Inc., an imprint of NordSüd Verlag AG,
CH-8005 Zürich, Switzerland.

Distributed in the United States by NorthSouth Books Inc., New York 10016.
Library of Congress Cataloging-in-Publication Data is available.

Printed in Germany by Grafisches Centrum Cuno GmbH & Co. KG, Calbe, May 2014.
ISBN: 978-0-7358-4175-8 (trade)
1 3 5 7 9 · 10 8 6 4 2

www.northsouth.com

Bernadette Watts

THE GOLDEN PLATE

North
South

Elisabeth had a Doll's House. It was beautiful. Flowering trees grew on either side of the Doll's House. In the hallway there was a telephone table and a telephone, doors leading into other rooms, and a staircase, with a blue carpet, going upstairs.

Elisabeth and her friend Isobel, who lived nearby, often played with the beautiful Doll's House.

Elisabeth sat the grandmother and grandfather dolls in chairs.
Isobel arranged a tea set on the kitchen table. Isobel took the lids off the tiny copper saucepans and put them on again. She looked at the round serving plate hanging on a nail over the stove. The plate was gold.

But the Doll's House belonged to Elisabeth, and everything in it belonged to Elisabeth.

Isobel took the golden plate off the nail. She slipped it into her pocket. "I must go home now, Elisabeth!"

Isobel walked home. The golden plate felt heavy in
her pocket. When she got home, the plate felt heavier.

Isobel also had a Doll's House, but it was not a real Doll's House. It used to be shelves for books. The golden plate from Elisabeth's Doll's House did not look so pretty in Isobel's Doll's House. It was too big! Too, too big . . . and ugly!

She pushed the plate under the pillow on her bed and went back downstairs.

"Don't you like your tea?" asked her mother.

"I'm not really hungry," said Isobel, staring at the golden cake.

When Isobel went to bed, she could feel the golden plate through her pillow—a huge hard lump. She could not shut her eyes.

She threw the plate across the dark room. Then she pulled the bedcover up so that she could not see where the plate lay on the floor.

The moon shone brightly through the window.

In the morning the little plate was in a corner.

The sun shone on the vegetable patch, on
the herbs growing in pots, and on the climbing
roses. Isobel dug a hole behind the rhubarb
clump and buried the plate.

It was a hot day. How bright the sun shone
on the golden sunflowers, their faces staring
intently at Isobel.

Isobel ran indoors where her mother was making lunch.

"I'm sorry! I'm sorry! I'm sorry!" Isobel wept.

Her mother held her tightly and listened to all she said. "The plate does not belong to you, Isobel. You must go and give it back to Elisabeth."

Isobel trudged along the road. The road seemed so steep today. The soles of her shoes were made of lead.

The afternoon was very hot. The golden plate burned in her pocket.

Isobel's mother watched through the front window and then made a telephone call.

Elisabeth and her parents were so pleased to see Isobel. They were waiting by the open front door.

"I have brought your plate back," said Isobel. "I am so sorry I took it."

"You can keep it if you like!" Elisabeth replied. "There are lots more exactly the same in the toyshop."

"No. It belongs to you."

The two friends hung the plate back on the nail. They played
with the dolls and rearranged the furniture.

They played a long time together.
Then Elisabeth and her mother walked Isobel back to her home.
It was evening; the air was fresh and gentle after the hot day.
Isobel was happy again.

A few months later it was Isobel's birthday. Her father had put a red roof on her Doll's House and a green lawn and little trees in front.

Isobel unwrapped her presents. There was a little piano, a painted table with matching chairs, and a brass clock.

Isobel was so happy.

In the afternoon Elisabeth came to tea. "Happy Birthday!
This is for you!" Elisabeth gave Isobel a tiny box.

Isobel undid the pretty ribbon very carefully. Inside
the box lay a tiny plate. It was gold.

And it was her own.